W9-BMP-216

tiny titans

STONE ARCH BOOKS
a capstone imprint

STONE ARCH BOOKS™

Published in 2012
A Capstone Imprint
1710 Roe Crest Drive
North Mankato, MN 56003
www.capstonepub.com

Originally published by DC Comics in the U.S. in
single magazine form as Tiny Titans #4.
Copyright © 2012 DC Comics. All Rights Reserved.

DC Comics
1700 Broadway, New York, NY 10019
A Warner Bros. Entertainment Company

Cataloging-in-Publication Data is available at the Library of
Congress website:
ISBN: 978-1-4342-4540-3 (library binding)

Summary: Find out what happens when Robin's life
goes to the birds! Plus, more Tiny fun than you
can shake a stick at!

STONE ARCH BOOKS

Ashley C. Andersen Zantop *Publisher*
Michael Dahl *Editorial Director*
Donald Lemke & Alison Deering *Editors*
Heather Kindseth *Creative Director*
Hilary Wacholz *Designer*
Kathy McColley *Production Specialist*

DC COMICS

Jann Jones *Original U.S. Editor*
Stephanie Buscema *U.S. Assistant Editor*
Nick J. Napolitano *Letterer*

Printed in the United States of America
in Brainerd, Minnesota.
122012 007078R

tiny titans

Enter: Nightwing!

By Eisner Winners
Art Baltazar & Franco

tiny titans

 CYBORG

 STARFIRE

 RAVEN

 KID FLASH

 MISS MARTIAN

 MAMMOTH

 TERRA

 BEAST BOY

 ROBIN

 WONDER GIRL

 BUMBLEBEE

 JERICHO

 ROSE

 SPEEDY

tiny titans

"ROBIN AND THE ROBINS"

RAVEN? DO YOU HAVE A BIRD PROBLEM TOO?

RAVENS ACTUALLY.

I DON'T KNOW WHAT TO DO!

tiny titans

"BABYSITTIN' BABY MAKEOVER!"

AW YEAH TITANS! LET'S PLAY BALL!

BUT WONDERGIRL, YOU CAN'T PLAY TODAY. IT'S YOUR TURN TO BABYSIT **THE LITTLE TINY TITANS.**

YEAH, SORRY.

AW, MAN! BUT... BUT... I...

THAT'S OKAY, WONDERGIRL. I'LL HELP YOU.

ALL RIGHT, WHAT DO WE HAVE TO DO?

WE HAVE TO MAKE SURE THE BABIES ARE **CLEAN.** AND, WE GOTTA CHANGE THEIR **CLOTHES.** AND, WE GOTTA **FEED** 'EM, TOO!

HMM... DOESN'T SEEM TOO DIFFICULT.

BABY SITTING RULES

WHAT THE HECK IS THIS?!

THAT'S WILDEBEEST. HE'S A NEW KID.

LI'L WIL, HUH?

SNIFF SNIFF SNIFF

PEEE--OOOOOO, WILLY! YOU'RE GONNA NEED SOME WORK!

RUB
BUF
BUFF
DRY
TO WEL

OKAY, WILLY, TIME TO GET CLEAN!

WHAT THE?

HE'S ALREADY CLEAN, WONDERGIRL. AND HE SMELLS GOOD TOO!

C'MON, BEE. LET'S GO GET HIM SOME CLEAN CLOTHES.

OKAY.

15

MEET THE... tiny titans

ROBIN

(Dick Grayson)- The brave and serious leader of the Tiny Titans. Although he is the original Robin, he is very moody and has to share his room with his brothers, the other Robins.
Also, he has secret crushes for Starfire and Barbara Gordon.

JASON TODDLER

The youngest of the three Robins. Too young to go to school, Jason is always in a happy mood and has a care-free style. He's all about smiling and having fun.

TIM DRAKE

The cool Robin. Tim wants to stand out from his brothers by wearing his own unique Robin costume. He's very laid back and easy going indeed.

KID FLASH

The super speedster and fasted kid in the school. Quick witted and eats lots for lunch because of his high metabolism. Too much candy will cause major sugar rush.

AQUALAD

The little boy from the ocean. Has a pet fish named Fluffy. Aqualad can communicate with all forms of sea life, even the pet hamster in their classroom.

SPEEDY

Quiet and cool, he is the boy with the trick arrows. He's good at anything that requires aiming. Also, he's Kid Flash's best friend.

WONDER GIRL

(Donna) Raised by amazons. She's strong and cute. Never lie to her, she has a magical jump rope which makes people tell the truth. Very skeptic.

RAVEN

The quiet and mysterious little girl. She really likes to experiment with dark magic, which usually turn into bad practical jokes. Mr. Trigon, the substitute teacher is her father.

CYBORG

Half boy, half robot. Cyborg is always tinkering with mechanical gadgets, often turning them into something else. His battle cry "BOO-YA!" has earned him the nickname, "Big Boo-Ya".

BEAST BOY

The green little boy who can change into any animal he desires. He's a prankster and loves comics. Has a crush on Terra.

STARFIRE

She's an alien princess. Very naïve and free spirited and finds the good in others. Has a crush on Robin and thinks he's cute, but so do all the other girls.

KID DEVIL

One of the younger Tiny Titans, still too young for school. Cannot talk but can breathe fire, usually while coughing or sneezing or hiccupping.

ROSE & JERICHO

Principal Slade's kids. Rose is the older and tougher "Tom-Boy" of the two. Jericho can't speak, but can take over your mind if you look into his eyes.

MISS MARTIAN

A shape shifting little girl alien from Mars who is still too young to go to school. She is often mistaken for Beast Boy's little sister.

TERRA

The sometimes hated little girl who likes to throw rocks. Principal Slade's teacher's pet. She thinks Beast Boy is a weirdo.

CASSIE

Wonder Girl's rich cousin from the big city. Cassie's really into fashion and is hip to all the latest trends in POP culture.

BUMBLE BEE

The tiniest of the Tiny Titans. BB buzzes and packs a mighty stinger.

Creators

Art Baltazar is a cartoonist machine from the heart of Chicago! He defines cartoons and comics not only as an art style, but as a way of life. Currently, Art is the creative force behind *The New York Times* best-selling, Eisner Award-winning, DC Comics series Tiny Titans, and the co-writer for Billy Batson and the Magic of SHAZAM! and co-creator of Superman Family Adventures. Art is living the dream! He draws comics and never has to leave the house. He lives with his lovely wife, Rose, big boy Sonny, little boy Gordon, and little girl Audrey. Right on!

ART BALTAZAR

FRANCO

Bronx, New York born writer and artist Franco Aureliani has been drawing comics since he could hold a crayon. Currently residing in upstate New York with his wife, Ivette, and son, Nicolas, Franco spends most of his days in a Batcave-like studio where he produces DC's Tiny Titans comics. In 1995, Franco founded Blindwolf Studios, an independent art studio where he and fellow creators can create children's comics. Franco is the creator, artist, and writer of Weirdsville, L'il Creeps, and Eagle All Star, as well as the co-creator and writer of Patrick the Wolf Boy. When he's not writing and drawing, Franco also teaches high school art.

Glossary

COSTUME [KOSS·toom] – clothes worn by people or actors in disguise

DIFFICULT [DIF·uh·kuhlt] – something that is not easy

EXHAUSTING [ig·ZAW·sting] – something that makes you very tired

FEARSOME [FIHR·suhm] – frightening

NERVOUS [NUR·vuhss] – fearful or timid

Action Accessories

Speedy

BOW AND ARROW

Robin

CAPE

Terra

ROCKS

Aqualad

FLUFFY

Wonder Girl

MAGIC JUMP ROPE

Visual Questions & Prompts

1. WHAT HAPPENS TO BEAST BOY WHEN HE GETS NERVOUS AT THE DENTIST? HOW CAN YOU TELL WHAT HE'S FEELING? TALK ABOUT WHAT YOU DO WHEN YOU'RE FEELING NERVOUS.

2. WHICH OF THE LITTLE TINY TITANS (IN THE PANEL BELOW) IS YOUR FAVORITE? WHY?

3. ROBIN AND RAVEN HAVE DIFFERENT APPROACHES TO THEIR BIRD PROBLEMS. WHY DO YOU THINK RAVEN WAS ABLE TO GET RID OF HER BIRDS AND ROBIN COULDN'T? TALK ABOUT SOME OTHER WAYS ROBIN COULD GET RID OF HIS BIRDS.

4. GRAPHIC NOVELS AND COMICS DON'T ALWAYS USE WORDS TO TELL A STORY. SOMETIMES ILLUSTRATIONS WORK JUST AS WELL. HOW DOES KID DEVIL HELP WILDEBEEST EVEN THOUGH THERE ARE NO WORDS?

tiny titans